THE BARNYARD SWITCH

D0557211

THE BARNYARD SWITCH

AND OTHER ANIMAL ESCAPADES
Compiled by the Editors
of
Highlights for Children

Compilation copyright © 1995 by Highlights for Children, Inc.
Contents copyright by Highlights for Children, Inc.
Published by Highlights for Children, Inc.
P.O. Box 18201
Columbus, Ohio 43218-0201
Printed in the United States of America

All rights reserved

ISBN 0-87534-641-3

Highlights° is a registered trademark of Highlights for Children, Inc.

CONTENTS

THE BARNYARD SWITCH

By Judith A. Enderle

"What a good life you lead, Rufus," said Plato, the pig. "I'll bet you can see the whole world from that fence post. If I could choose," said Plato, "I would rather be a rooster."

"Nonsense, Plato!" said Rufus. "True, I can see a lot up here. But the one who leads a good life is Duncan, the dog. He has a soft rug and food served in a dish. If I could choose," said Rufus, the rooster, "I would rather be a dog."

"You are wrong, Rufus," said Duncan, the dog. "Look at Plato. He rolls in the mud and no one scolds him for being dirty. He gets more to eat than you or I. If I could choose, I would be a pig," said Duncan.

Plato looked at Rufus. Rufus looked at Duncan. Duncan looked at Plato. "Let's switch!" they said.

That night Rufus slept on Duncan's rug by the door. Duncan snored in Plato's pigpen. And Plato watched the sky by the fence post.

Soon the stars faded. "I'd better get ready to crow," said Plato. He looked up. *How will I get up to the fence post?* he wondered. *I have no wings.* He thought for a minute. "I will have to climb," he said.

Plato grunted and groaned. He lifted one leg, then the other. He stretched and twisted. His roly-poly body shook. His short legs wobbled. Finally, he rested his front feet halfway up the fence post.

"I'm standing!" he cried. "But I can't see the world. I can't even see all of the barnyard. I must sit on top of the post."

He took a deep breath. He bent his knees. "One, two, three," he counted. Plato jumped.

"Oomph!" He landed tummy first right on top of the fence post. He rocked forward. He rocked backward. He couldn't catch hold with his feet. Below him the ground tipped up and down, up and down.

"Oh, I can't sit up. I can't climb down. I'm dizzy." Then he noticed the brightness around him. "The sun is coming up," he groaned. "I'd better crow. OINK-A-DOODLE DOO! OINK-A-DOODLE DOO! OINK-A-DOODLE HELP!" squealed Plato as he lost his balance and fell from the fence post.

On the porch Rufus the rooster stretched. "Sleeping on a rug by the door is very pleasant," he said. "But I'm hungry. I should let the farmer's wife know. Then she will bring me some food." He ruffled his feathers and stretched his neck. "COCK-A-DOODLE WOOF! COCK-A-DOODLE WOOF!"

Wham! The front door hit him in the tail.

"COCK-A-DOODLE OOF!" crowed Rufus. He flew into the bushes. A robin flew up and scolded. Flower blossoms and leaves clung to his feathers.

"What's wrong with that rooster?" cried Farmer Pumpernickel. "He sounds sick." He didn't even notice Rufus as he ran down the front steps, nightshirt flapping behind him.

Rufus picked himself up. "Two of my most beautiful tail feathers are bent," he cried. "They took me such a long time to grow, too." He flew back up onto the porch.

Out the door raced the Pumpernickel children.

"DOODLE WOOF!" cried Rufus, flapping out of the way just in time.

9

"Don't forget your chores," called Farmer Pumpernickel. He went back into the house shaking his head. "I must have been dreaming that awful sound," he said.

Finally, Mrs. Pumpernickel came out. She placed a large bone in the dog dish.

"I'm so hungry," said Rufus. "This is much better than pecking and poking about in the dirt." He opened his beak wide to pick up the bone. It didn't move. "Too heavy," he said. "I shall take little bites." *CLICK CLICK* went his beak as he pecked at the bone. "I can't eat this," crowed Rufus. "My beak is too small. I don't have the sharp teeth that Duncan has."

In the pigpen Duncan rolled about in the mud. "GRRR-UNT! GRRR-UNT! This is fun," he said.

Then he heard the Pumpernickel children. He raced over to the fence to be petted. "GRR-UNT!" he called. The children passed right by.

"I guess I forgot," said Duncan. "The children don't play with Plato." He looked down at his fur. "And they probably couldn't see me anyway. I blend with the mud." He felt very lonely. He put his head back and howled.

Duncan's tail drooped when Plato limped over to the pigpen. "Hello, Duncan," he said. "You were right. It is better to be a pig. I would rather be me."

"No, Plato. Rufus was right," said Duncan. He shook mud in all directions. "It is better to be a dog. I'd rather be me."

Rufus flew to the top of the fence post. "No, no," he said. "Plato was right. It is definitely better to be a rooster. I'd rather be me."

"Let's switch back!" they said. "We are all right. It is better to be yourself!"

MR. GOAT'S BAD GOOD IDEA

By Marileta Robinson

One morning Mr. Goat was finishing the roof on his new hogan. "Oh, bugs and butter," he said. "I don't have enough mud to finish the roof."

At first he thought he would have to dig up some dirt to make more mud. *But,* he thought to himself, *that's the hard way. I know an easy way. Mr. Prairie Dog is always digging holes. He probably has some dirt he will be glad to give me. I'll just walk over there and see.*

13

Mr. Prairie Dog was sitting at the door of his hole in the ground. There was a big pile of dirt beside him. "Good morning, Mr. Goat," he said. "Look at all this dirt. I just finished digging out a new room in my house."

"What do you know!" said Mr. Goat. "I was just coming to ask you for some dirt to make some mud. I don't have enough mud to finish the roof of my new hogan."

"Well, I was going to make some mud to put on the walls of my new room. But if you will get me some rabbit fur to put in my bed, I'll let you have some dirt."

"That won't be too much trouble," said Mr. Goat, and he set off for Mrs. Rabbit's place, saying, "Rabbit fur, rabbit fur," so he wouldn't forget. Mrs. Rabbit was in front of her hogan, making frybread. She was dropping flat pieces of dough into a pan of hot oil and letting them puff up brown and crisp.

"Here, Mr. Goat," she said, giving him a piece of hot frybread.

"Thank you," said Mr. Goat. After he had finished eating the frybread, he said, "Do you have any rabbit fur you could give me, Mrs. Rabbit?"

"Yes, I do have some," said Mrs.Rabbit. "I just finished brushing the children's coats and I have a nice big pile of it. I was going to use it to weave a rug. But if you will get me some fresh heads of lettuce, I will let you have some fur."

"Well, that won't be too much trouble, I guess," said Mr. Goat, and he walked over to the trading post saying, "Lettuce, rabbit fur, lettuce, rabbit fur."

There were lots of people in the trading post wanting to buy things. While he waited, Mr. Goat had plenty of time to look around at the lanterns, plates, ropes, coffee pots, and the big iron stove. Finally, it was his turn. "I want some lettuce," he said to the trader.

"How many heads?" said the trader. "It's thirty cents a head."

"Wa-hah!" said Mr. Goat in surprise. "I forgot, I don't have any money! May I trade you something for the lettuce?"

"OK," said the trader. "Bring me some wool and I'll give you some lettuce."

So Mr. Goat walked over to Mr. Sheep's house saying, "Wool, lettuce, rabbit fur, lool, fluttuce, rabbit fur, rool, rabbit, lettuce fur."

Mr. Sheep was sitting in the sun. When he saw Mr. Goat, he said, "Sit down over here, Mr. Goat. You look very tired."

"No, I can't sit down," said Mr. Goat. "I wish I could. But I have to take some wool to the trader. Do you have any you could give me?"

"Yes," said Mr. Sheep. "I have some. I was going to sell it to the trader myself, but if you will bring me some fresh hay, I'll give you some wool."

So Mr. Goat walked over to Mr. Horse's farm. He was too tired to say anything but, "Hay, hay, hay."

"What's the matter, Mr. Goat?" said Mr. Horse, who was working in his field.

"Nothing," said Mr. Goat, "except that I need some hay. Can you give me some?"

"Why, Mr. Goat!" said Mr. Horse, looking worried. "Do you need food?"

"No, no, it's not for me. I have to give some hay to Mr. Sheep."

"Why?"

"He's going to give me some wool for it."

"Oh, I see. You want to weave a blanket."

"No, I'm going to give the wool to the trader so he will give me some lettuce."

"Then you do need food!"

"No, the lettuce is for Mrs. Rabbit."

"Why are you getting lettuce for Mrs. Rabbit?" asked Mr. Horse, scratching his head.

Mr. Goat sighed. "It's very simple. If I give Mrs. Rabbit the lettuce, she will give me some rabbit fur. If I give the rabbit fur to Mr. Prairie Dog, he will give me some dirt. Then I can make some mud and finish the roof of my new hogan."

"If you needed dirt, why didn't you dig it yourself?" asked Mr. Horse.

"That's not so easy to explain," said Mr. Goat. "Please may I have some hay?"

"Well," said Mr. Horse, "I can see you like to trade. If you will fix the pump on my windmill, I'll give you some hay."

Mr. Goat took some tools and banged and twisted and wiggled the pump until it was fixed.

"Thank you," said Mr. Horse, and he gave Mr. Goat a big basket of hay.

"Thank you," said Mr. Goat, and he started down the road. "Let's see," he said. "First I take the hay to the trader and he will give me some wool. No, that's not right. First I take the hay to Mrs. Rabbit and she will give me some lettuce. No, that's not right either!"

Poor Mr. Goat sat down on the basket of hay and took some deep breaths until he got it all straight. Then he took the hay to Mr. Sheep and got some wool.

He took the wool to the trader and got two heads of lettuce.

He took the lettuce to Mrs. Rabbit and got some rabbit fur (and another piece of frybread).

Then he took the rabbit fur to Mr. Prairie Dog, and Mr. Prairie dog gave him a big bucket of dirt.

By the time Mr. Goat got home, the sun was just going down behind the hogan. He was covered with dust and too sore and tired to work on his roof. Mr. Goat thought to himself, *I'm not so sure that was really the easy way.*

Terrible Teddy, the Unbearable Bear

By Nancy West

Our teacher says that all of us bears are very smart and lots of fun. But it's been hard to feel glad about our class, because Terrible Teddy is in it.

He's new in our school, and we never really noticed him—except when he caused trouble.

If he got to school on time, it was a miracle.

If he ever played nicely on the swings, it was another miracle.

And if he painted without flinging painty water from the tip of his brush, Ms. Duncan was amazed.

One Tuesday I came back from feeding the goldfish and found out when I sat down that someone had put a tack on my chair.

Ow! I jumped and turned to glare at Terrible Teddy, who rolled his eyes at me.

Later, Teddy squirted water on Lorraine. Then he bragged about his cooking and burned the bread we were baking for the Old Bears' Home. And laughed about it!

That was the last straw for Ms. Duncan. She said, "Teddy, I want you to practice your writing while we finish this work."

"I don't want to practice my writing," Teddy said.

"Practice anyway," said Ms. Duncan, who was standing with her hands on her hips. We all knew that she meant business.

He went to his seat, pulled out a pen, and knocked four books to the floor before he started.

We baked more bread, wrapped it in wax paper, went outside for recess, came back in, washed our hands, did arithmetic, and sang "Oh, My Darling Clementine," and Terrible was still writing.

"Take it home now, Teddy, and bring it back tomorrow," Ms. Duncan said. He gathered up his papers and left.

When we walked home, there was no sign of Teddy. He wasn't hiding behind the schoolhouse ready to jump out and cause trouble. He didn't sneak up behind us and throw things like snowballs and pebbles at us.

The next day at school Terrible Teddy was sitting at his desk, his tongue sticking out of one side of his mouth, still writing.

"Goodness," Ms. Duncan said. "Aren't you finished yet, Teddy?"

"Soon," he said.

We did our schoolwork, and we kept waiting for Teddy to fall on the floor laughing, to tease little Leo, to pull Lorraine's hair, to throw spitballs at me, to yank leaves off Pansy's plant, or to hide Willis's pencils. But he didn't.

Finally he put his pen down. There was silence as the scratching of pen on paper stopped.

Ms. Duncan picked up his papers and read the first page. She got a funny look on her face. "I'll read this out loud," she said and cleared her throat.

"Once upon a time," she read, "there was a smart and beautiful princess named Lorraine. She was the favorite of her father, the king, and he took her along when he went to visit other kingdoms. All the kings in the land loved Lorraine. She was proud, and she had her very own horse."

We all looked at Lorraine, who was smiling happily. "Wow!" she said. "I *love* that story."

Ms. Duncan started reading again. "Once a very small bear named Leo was sad because he was not as big as his friends. Sometimes he got tears in his eyes just thinking about it."

We all looked at Leo. He had tears in his eyes.

"But one day a baby bear fell into a deep, narrow well. They needed someone small enough to save the baby, and Leo came running. He put grease all over himself and tied a rope around his waist and went down the dark, clammy well. In a few minutes, he came back up with the baby. The baby was safe, thanks to Leo."

Everyone in our class yelled and pounded Leo on the back, as if it had been a real baby.

I looked at Terrible Teddy, but he just sat with his hands folded, listening as if he was hearing the stories for the first time.

There was a story about Pansy, who became a famous florist and sent flowers to the White House every day, and one about Willis, who became a famous Senator bear and grew a beard down to his belt buckle.

And there was one about me, Benjamin Bear. I baked a cake as big as a city block, and my picture was in the paper, and I won a ticket to a bake-off in Paris, France, where I won first prize for my chocolate torte!

There was a story about everyone in the class. There was even one about Ms. Duncan, who was an angel of mercy flying all over the world doing good deeds. Ms. Duncan sniffled at the end of the story and said she'd keep it forever.

She picked up the last story. "Once upon a time there was a bear who was in trouble most of the time. It was always his own fault. But he couldn't seem to stop being bad, because when he was in trouble, everyone paid attention to him and he didn't have to be alone."

I looked at Lorraine. She looked at Willis. He looked at Leo.

Ms. Duncan read more; "But one day he sat down and wrote some stories, and when he got started, he couldn't stop. It was the most fun he ever had. Does he grow up to be a famous writer? He sure hopes so."

I got a lump in my throat. Poor Terrible. He just wanted to be noticed. But he went about it wrong.

No one said anything for a long time. I guess we were thinking about what we should do.

Then I said, "Terrible—I mean, Teddy—come over after school, and we'll go honey-hunting in the logs down by the river."

"Wait!" Lorraine said. "I want you to come with me and watch the sun go down over the pond."

Ms. Duncan asked if Teddy would like to write the school play. He said he would. It was a nice morning, and we all felt glowy and good inside.

When we left school that day, Teddy jumped out from behind the building. "Boo!" he shouted.

We all laughed and walked home together. Teddy's a very smart bear, and he's lots of fun.

The Education of Seymour DeFrige

By Linell Wohlers

Seymour DeFrige was well hidden in his mouse-hole behind the refrigerator. Humans who used the refrigerator had an "outside only cat" who seldom saw the kitchen. Mousetraps never appeared because he left no mouse damage.

Seymour was mostly free to pursue his favorite hobby, reading. He had learned to read from school papers, which clung by magnet to the refrigerator. The feast of reading on that door had nourished his mind, just as the crumb feast on the floor had nourished his body.

When he wasn't stockpiling spilled food, Seymour was reading. When human life entered the kitchen, he'd retire to his mousehole to think while his food digested.

He enjoyed food words on grocery lists and diets, and a sign that said THINK THIN! He wondered about school buses and vacations when he read the PTA calendar. He loved cartoons, especially the cat with its clever word balloons. But he really looked forward to the school papers written by Terry Kramer. Through these pages he had first received the gift of reading. Now they brought him ideas about oceans, constellations, electricity, maps, and animals.

But one spring day, things started changing. Track Day ribbons and notices for "The End-of-School Picnic" went up. School papers came down. Constant human activity barely gave Seymour a chance to grab a meal and squeeze back under the refrigerator before footsteps returned. Floors were swept. Cupboards slammed. The refrigerator opened and shut a thousand times.

"Find the swimsuits!"

"Load the cooler!"

"Grab that suitcase!"

Suddenly the house was quiet. There were no humans to trouble him and plenty of crumbs the broom had missed. But as days passed, another hunger grew inside Seymour DeFrige. The refrigerator door contained nothing to read except old grocery lists, a calendar page labeled "Summer Vacation" and a painful reminder to THINK THIN!

Before he realized it, Seymour had chewed off the corner of a cookbook, trying to get to the words inside. He had squeezed into cupboards where cereal boxes offered new reading. (And, as he discovered, new snacking!) Colorful canisters on the counter beckoned him with food words. Seymour was just scaling them when suddenly the backdoor flew open.

"Hold the door!"

"Hang those jackets!"

"What's to eat?"

With no time to think, Seymour ran for the refrigerator, terrified by human shouts and footsteps. From his mousehole he watched a broomstick rattle under the refrigerator to scare him out of hiding. When mouse damage was discovered, a mousetrap was set!

Fortunately, Seymour sprang the trap. Unlike most mice who go for the cheese end, he was more interested in the end with writing on it.

Next, the "outdoor only cat" was invited into the kitchen. Seymour found him even more clever than the cartoon cat! There was no hope of eating or reading now. He waited till the cat was put out to make his escape to the outside world.

The high ceiling of sky and moving air frightened Seymour. But he soon realized how much there was to eat and read. Discarded food containers offered excellent mouse dining and a menu to read!

Life as a vagabond was appealing, but something else was happening, too. A real education was beginning for Seymour. Crumb-scrounging trips through the zoo brought him face-to-face with animals he had only read about.

Nights of glorious camping at the foot of a billboard introduced him to the nighttime sky. Instantly he knew the Big Dipper from reading about constellations on the refrigerator back home.

He experienced firsthand how lightning was one kind of electricity and the glow from buildings, signs, and streetlights was another.

He found that everything in the real City Park matched Terry Kramer's map of City Park.

One evening at sunset, Seymour found his way to some leftovers around a beach concession stand. A rhythmic roar called him over the sand dunes. He watched, quivering with wonder as wave after wave came to crash on the shore. Reading about the ocean is one thing, but seeing it is quite another!

Months of adventure passed while Seymour watched his reading come to life.

One chilly morning he was drawn through an open door to warmth and the smell of food. As he was chewing his way into a bag of groceries, Seymour felt his new shelter rumble and roll! He was puzzled until he remembered something he'd read. So this was a bus!

When the bus stopped, Seymour DeFrige had no choice but to keep still and wait. As his hiding place was jostled about, he wondered what adventure awaited him next.

When the grocery bag came to rest in a solid quiet place, Seymour chewed his way out to look around. Amazed and delighted, he once again stood before the refrigerator, loaded with school papers! Terry Kramer had been writing about mountains, computers, presidents, spaceships, and something called photosynthesis. There was "Back-To-School-Night" on the calendar, a yogurt diet to help someone THINK THIN!, a long grocery list, and new cartoons. Miraculously, he was home!

Seymour quickly settled back into this life of eating and reading. But he remembered with exquisite twinges the past adventures that had brought meaning to all he'd read. The next time that "Summer Vacation" flashed across the refrigerator, Seymour DeFrige was ready to travel. He would always love reading at home, but he had discovered that reading was only the beginning of his education.

False Friend Finchley

By M. Donnaleen Howitt

In a small muddy swamp lived three little frogs, Finchley, Forbes, and Franco.

It was not a very nice swamp. The water was shallow and thick with mud.

"Someday," said Forbes, "I'll leave this old swamp and find a better place."

"Before you do," said Finchley, "show me how you hop so far and catch insects so quickly."

"Of course, friend Finchley," said Forbes. "I'll be glad to show you, but I would like to be on my way soon."

"Me too!" said Franco, in his deep, deep voice.

"But you must not leave," said Finchley. "Not before you teach me to sing as sweetly as you do."

"Surely," said Franco. "I will give you singing lessons, but the days are growing short and I must not delay."

Forbes's legs grew tired and sore as he showed Finchley again and again how to crouch low and push himself forward, springing high and far in the pond. Then they practiced tongue-flicking, until Finchley could catch insects in a flash.

Franco spent many hours teaching his friend Finchley to take in great gulps of air and let them out slowly in deep, musical *gaah-RUMPHS*. Their throaty songs echoed through the swamp, thrilling the other frogs.

Early one day Finchley hopped away, without so much as a "good-bye" or a "thanks."

The next day the little swamp was covered with frost, and the lily pads were icy.

"It's too late for us to leave," said Forbes with a sigh. "It took so long to teach Finchley everything that now we must wait for spring."

Finchley hopped south, to a pond where the frost had not yet come. When the frogs there saw him hop and heard him sing, they were amazed. Soon he became a very important frog indeed.

"Teach us to hop and sing as well as you do," cheeped all the young frogs as they sat in a crowd admiring Finchley.

"Keep the pond clean. Scrub the lily pads. Catch insects for my supper. And always call me Sir Finchley," he commanded. "Then perhaps I will teach you." Finchley flicked his tongue at a firefly, then dozed on a large lily pad.

In the spring, after a long, cold winter, Forbes and Franco left their muddy little swamp. They traveled south, and one night they heard a frog singing in the twilight.

"That's Finchley's voice," said Franco. "We have found our old friend."

In a while they saw Finchley sitting in a pretty little pond, surrounded by frogs who were waiting on him and admiring him.

"Hello, old friend," said Forbes. "I'm so glad we found you."

"Why are you here?" demanded Finchley. He was not pleased to see them.

"We've come to enjoy the pond with you, to sing with you, and to hop with you, just as we once did," said Franco.

"I am much too important to bother with you now," said Finchley. "Besides, you talk and look like muddy swamp frogs. Please leave my pond."

Forbes was so startled that he hopped all the way from a lily pad to the shore.

"Look at that leap!" the little frogs said. "Why, he's the greatest leaper in the world!"

Franco felt so sad about the change in his old friend that he began to sing, *gaah-RUMPHing* in his deep, deep voice.

"Did you hear him sing?" the frogs asked each other. "That's the sweetest voice we've ever heard. Come on everybody, let's follow the new frogs. We can learn a lot from them!"

All the little frogs followed Forbes and Franco, who searched around and soon found a lovely pond with tall bullrushes and shiny lily pads. They taught the little frogs to hop farther, sing better, and catch more insects. In the evenings they all sang happily together.

One day, just at dusk, they paused in their singing and heard a faint, froggy voice from a nearby pond. It was Finchley.

"Come back, come back," he sang as the sun disappeared.

"No thanks, no thanks," the young frogs cheeped.

"How could you leave a good friend like me?" Finchley sang softly.

The big and little frogs took in a great gulp of air and sang a song Franco had taught them:

A friend will always help you,
A friend is always fair.
A friend is glad to see you,
No matter when or where.
We share the work and insects,
We play together, too.
When you learn what friendship is,
We'll make room for you!

The frogs listened in the darkness. Only the chirping crickets broke the silence. Then they heard Finchley's voice, growing much closer.

"I'll learn, I'll learn, I'll learn," sang Finchley.

The Little UHO

By Joyce Mikkola

When Mother Hen felt a slight movement beneath her, she jumped quickly off the nest. She looked closely at the eggs. Here and there were tiny cracks.

"Oh," she clucked happily, "this is the day my chicks will come out of their shells!"

She looked around the barnyard. "But what will they eat? They cannot eat large grains of corn like the grown chickens do or the things they feed the piglets! I shall have to go to the farmhouse and bring back some of the very fine meal that is put in the yard for the goslings!"

She started away toward the yard. "I shall hurry and be back when they come out of their shells," she said to herself.

Now, the baby chicks knew it was time to jump out of their shells and meet their mother for the first time. So, pecking away, soon one, then two, then three, and on and on until eleven chicks were out of their shells.

Each one hopped out of the nest but stayed close to it and to each other. All started crying for their mother.

Now only one egg was left in the nest. The baby chick inside this shell was smaller than the others. He was much shorter. His little beak could not peck out a large opening up high as the other chicks had done.

I shall do the best I can, thought the baby chick, and he pecked and pecked. Finally, the bottom part of the eggshell separated completely from the top part.

The baby chick stepped out of the bottom part of the shell, but he couldn't get the top part off him, so he jumped out of the nest anyway, like the other chicks had done. He wanted to be with them when they met their mother.

When he came near, the chicks ran away.

"Look!" cried one. "What is that?"

Baby Chick couldn't see what they meant, because his shell covered him like a tent umbrella, leaving only his skinny little legs visible.

"I think it must be a walking mushroom," said a young turkey.

"Oh, no," said Piglet, who was almost grown and had once been to market and back. "I think it must be a UFO!"

"Well," said the duckling, "since you know so much, whatever is a UFO?"

Piglet looked about. Everyone was listening.

"A UFO is something that flies about, and no one knows what it is. So whenever anyone sees something that is flying and they aren't sure what it is, that is what they call it!"

"But what does UFO mean?" asked the duckling.

"It means un-i-dent-i-fied flying object! That is the same as a don't-know-what flying object!"

"But this object is not flying! It is hopping!"

"That is true, duckling. So of course, that is a U*HO!* An un-i-dent-i-fied *hopping* object!"

All this time Baby Chick was trying to get rid of his shell, hoping he could do it in time to see the UHO. The more he hopped, the more in a tizzy the barnyard became.

"All we can be sure of at this time is that this is something from outer space!" Piglet puffed out his jowls and looked very wise.

Now Mother Hen had reached the farmhouse yard, found the goslings fine meal, and was rushing back to her nest. The nearer she came, the more alarmed she grew.

"What is happening?" she called out.

"Your chicks have hatched, and they are in grave danger!" shouted young Piglet.

Hearing this, Mother Hen ran very fast. When she reached her chicks, she spread her wings wide, and eleven baby chicks ran under them. Mother Hen held her chicks close.

"What is the danger?" the worried hen cried.

"There!" Piglet pointed to number twelve chick hopping helter-skelter under his shell, only his skinny little legs showing.

"There before you, Mother Hen, is the danger— a UHO!"

"What in the world are you talking about? *What* is a UHO?" asked Mother Hen.

Importantly, Piglet explained. "That is an unidentified hopping object! It is called that because no one really knows what it is, but everyone knows it's a danger!"

Mother Hen glared at Piglet.

"Really!" she said. She walked over and gave a sharp rap on the top of the shell. The shell broke into many pieces, and there, in all his smallness, stood chick number twelve!

"*There's* your dangerous hopping object!" she scolded the noisy gathering. She made room for the small chick under her wings and began dishing out the fine meal.

"How could I be so wrong?" Piglet wondered as he slipped away. "After all, I *have* been to market!"

The Curious Coyote

By Hariett Richie

In a wide canyon in the West lived a young coyote who liked chasing the wind, eating cactus blossoms, and sniffing new smells. And every evening he would climb to the top of a rocky ledge and watched the sun set behind the rim of the canyon.

"Where do you think the sun goes?" he asked the other coyotes. "It disappears on one side of the canyon, and the next morning it's on the other side. How does it do that?"

"Who cares?" one coyote said.

"Why do you want to know?" another asked.

"I'm curious. That's why," he said.

The next day, when the wind was still and he had eaten his fill of cactus blossoms, the young coyote climbed up the canyon. On a cliff near the top, a large bird was sitting on a nest. The young coyote wagged his tail. "Hello," he said. "What kind of bird are you?"

"A bald eagle," she replied, ruffling her feathers. "And you are a young coyote."

"That's right," he answered. "The wind smells different up here. I like to chase the wind."

"Ha! You're wasting your time," said the eagle. "I can fly, and I can't catch the wind." She flapped her wings. "You don't belong up here."

"Oh yes," the young coyote assured the eagle. "I'm trying to learn where the sun goes at the end of the day."

"Well, you won't find out up here," she scolded.

The young coyote backed away slowly. "I'll be on my way," he said.

A forest stood in the distance above the canyon, and the young coyote hurried to get a closer look. He was sniffing through some fallen leaves when he bumped into a cottonwood tree. A furry animal was hanging by her tail from a limb. The young coyote turned his head to the side. "Excuse me. Why are you hanging upside down?" he asked.

"I'm supposed to hang upside down. I'm a possum," she answered, swinging back and forth.

The young coyote moved closer. "Do you think that I could do that?"

"Are you kidding? You can't hang by your tail," the possum answered. She closed her eyes.

"Well, I'll be on my way," the young coyote said.

He found a trail through the forest. As he followed it, a strange smell became stronger and stronger. Soon he met a small black animal with a white stripe and a bushy tail that stuck almost straight up in the air.

"Hello," the coyote called. "Have you noticed a strange smell?"

The animal stared at him. "You don't know what that smell is? It's me. I'm a skunk. And it's not a strange smell. It stinks!"

"Oh no. It's not so bad once you get used to it. I like new smells," the young coyote assured him.

"You're not supposed to like it. It's the way I protect myself," the skunk said. "Now I'm getting out of here." And he ran into the woods.

"Oh my," the young coyote said to himself. "Maybe it isn't wise to be curious." He was thirsty, so he started back toward the wide canyon.

Near the river, an animal was gnawing into a thick tree trunk. Wood chips were flying everywhere. The animal had huge teeth, and his tail was as round and flat as a cactus plant. The young coyote was curious, but he did not say anything. The longer he watched, the more curious he became. Finally, he blurted out, "Excuse me, but you're amazing. Who are you?"

The animal stood on his hind legs and leaned back on his tail. "I'm a beaver, and I'm building a lodge. I don't remember seeing you around here. Who are you?"

"I'm a coyote from the canyon," he answered.

"A coyote," the beaver repeated. "Tell me about yourself. And how about pushing a few of those sticks over here? I could use some help."

"You could?" The young coyote picked up a stick between his teeth and dropped it on a pile near the bank.

"Thanks," the beaver said. "I'm trying to finish my work early so I can watch the sun disappear. I can't figure out how it disappears on one side of the river and the next morning it's on the other side."

"That's what I want to know!" the young coyote exclaimed. He rolled a small log with his nose and sniffed the roly-poly worms under it. "Tell me, Beaver, are you curious about other things?"

"Sure," the beaver answered. "I'd like to know how fish stay underwater all the time and what it would feel like to bite into the moon. But you haven't told me about yourself, Coyote."

"Well, I like eating cactus blossoms, sniffing new smells, and chasing the wind," he said. "And I'd like to know about building this lodge. It's really something."

"OK," the beaver said, starting back to work. "If you help me, we should have plenty of time for talking and watching the sun disappear. Maybe together we can figure out where it goes."

"Great," the young coyote said, dropping another stick on the pile. "And another thing, Beaver. I'm curious. What do you think about skunks?"

Bear Can't Find His Glasses

By Margaret Shoop

Bear woke up thinking about breakfast. He yawned and stretched in his king-size bed. Then he reached over to the nightstand for his glasses. His big paw found the lamp—and nothing else. "I was sure I put them there," he muttered.

Bear got up from bed and started to look through the house for his glasses. He wasn't worried. He was sure he would find them. He made up a song to sing while he searched:

*"I don't need my glasses for climbing
  up trees,
Or eating the honey I take from the bees,
Or catching a fish from a bubbly brook,
But I must wear my glasses when I read
  a book!"*

Bear looked everywhere. He found Mouse asleep under some old clothes in a closet. He found Cricket chirping behind a curtain. But he didn't find the missing glasses. A scowl came over his furry face. He had started a new book. He wanted to read more of the story at breakfast. "I must have left those glasses somewhere yesterday," he mumbled.

Bear sat down in his rocking chair. Back and forth went the rocker, while he tried to remember everything about the day before. Soon he said in a loud voice, "I'll bet I left them at Squirrel's house!"

Bear ran out the back door. He ran all the way to Squirrel's tree. Fox and Raccoon were visiting Squirrel. All three sat on the ground near the tree.

Bear was so upset that he forgot to say hello to everybody. He looked at Squirrel and said, "Did I happen to leave my glasses here? I can't find them anywhere at home."

Squirrel looked hard at Bear, and Bear saw a grin grow big on her face. Squirrel answered,

"Your glasses aren't here, Bear." Then she giggled and said, "Maybe you put them in a shoe."

In a cross voice Bear replied, "That's a silly idea, Squirrel. You know I don't wear shoes."

Fox burst out laughing and said, "Well, if you didn't put them in a shoe, then maybe they fell into your stew!"

Bear didn't eat stew. In a grumpy voice he said, "What's the matter with you two?"

Bear turned to Raccoon. Raccoon was lying on his back, holding his stomach, and laughing hard. Bear was annoyed with this, but he asked, "Have you seen my glasses, Raccoon? I was over at your place yesterday."

Raccoon seemed to have a hard time trying to talk. Finally, he took a deep breath and said, "Did you put them in a pocket, Bear?"

Fox snickered and said, "Or maybe they went up with a rocket."

Bear didn't have pockets, and Fox was being ridiculous again. In a grouchy voice Bear said, "You're not funny at all, Fox. In fact, none of you are funny. I think I'll take a walk."

Bear was upset. He growled a giant-sized growl as he stomped through the woods. He walked for a long time. Thinking. Trying to remember anything that would help him find his glasses. Wondering about the strange things his friends had asked. Wondering why they thought it was so funny that he couldn't find his glasses. Finally, Bear thought of Owl. She was good at solving problems. Maybe she could help solve this one.

Bear ran into the deep woods to Owl's tree. She was perched on a high branch. Bear yelled, "Wake up, Owl. Please!"

Owl woke up and fluttered down to a lower branch. Who could sleep when a bear was shouting? She moved quietly, almost like a moth. She settled herself on the branch and looked at Bear with her big yellow eyes. "What's the matter with you?" she asked. She sounded sleepy and grumpy.

Bear moaned, "I can't find my glasses, and I've looked everywhere I can think of."

Owl stared. She began to laugh. She kept on laughing. She laughed so hard that her feathers shook, and her ear tufts seemed to get bigger. Finally, she said, "Oh, my, you're such an absent-minded bear. Your glasses are on your head, pushed up into your fur."

Bear reached up with a paw and touched the missing glasses. He felt silly, but it didn't matter. The important thing was that his glasses were found. He knew what had happened. He had been reading his new book in bed and had fallen asleep with his glasses on. While he slept, they had been pushed up into his fur.

"Thank you, Owl. Thanks a lot," said Bear. Then he galloped home to read and have breakfast. As he ran, he laughed at himself and he sang:

> *"I did not put them in a shoe.*
> *They did not fall into my stew.*
> *I did not stick them in a pocket.*
> *They did not go up with a rocket.*
> *I wore them while I read in bed,*
> *And they got stuck upon my head."*

When Bear got home, there was a big note on his back door. It was signed by Squirrel, Fox, and Raccoon, and it said, "Hope you found your glasses. If you didn't, look in a mirror. We love you, Bear, but it *is* April Fools' Day!"

Rusty Rooster's Barnyard Parade

By Marilyn Kratz

"Cock-a-doodle-doo! A cheery good morning to you," crowed Rusty Rooster early one bright summer morning.

He flew down from the top of the fence and said to himself, "It's a perfect day for doing something special. Now what would I like to do that's special? I know! I'll lead a parade, and I'll ask all the farm animals to be in it."

Rusty ran to the barnyard. The first animal he saw was Pamela Palomino munching her breakfast hay.

"Cock-a-doodle-doo! A cheery good morning to you, Pamela Palomino," crowed Rusty. "Would you like to be in my parade?"

"**Neigh**borly of you to ask me," neighed Pamela. "I love parades. Of course I must lead it. Horses always lead a parade."

Oh, well, Rusty thought, *being second in a parade is almost being first. And Pamela Palomino would look lovely leading the parade.*

So he said to Pamela, "We'll meet in the meadow at noon. See you there."

As Rusty was leaving the barnyard, he met Cora Cow just coming in to get her breakfast.

"Cock-a-doodle-doo! A cheery good morning to you," crowed Rusty. "Please come to the meadow at noon and be in my parade."

"A parade? Well, now, I'm in the **moo**d for a parade. But I don't see so well anymore, so I'll have to lead the parade. Then I won't need to worry about staying in line because everyone will have to stay in line with me."

Rusty couldn't say no to nice old Cora Cow, so he said, "That's a fine idea."

Waddling across the barnyard came Delia Duck and her seven babies.

"Cock-a-doodle-doo! A cheery good morning to you," crowed Rusty. "There's going to be a grand parade in the meadow at noon today. Will you and your ducklings join in it?"

"**Qua**-n't," quacked Delia. "My ducklings could never keep up with a fast parade."

"We'll try not to go too fast," Rusty assured her.

"I was just thinking," said Delia Duck, "If my ducklings and I lead the parade, we won't have to worry about keeping up with the others. They'll have to go at our speed. Yes, we'll be in the parade if we can be first in line."

Poor Rusty! He didn't know what he was going to do. How could there be a parade if all the animals insisted on leading it?

Next he found Percy Pig dozing in a big, oozy mud puddle.

"Cock-a-doodle-doo! A cheery good morning to you," crowed Rusty. "Do you think you'll be dried out from your mud bath in time to join us in the meadow at noon today for a parade? Pamela Palomino and Cora Cow and Delia Duck and all her ducklings will be there."

"Oh, Rusty," oinked Percy, "I'm very **oink**-shus to be in a parade. But I'm not tall enough to see over Pamela Palomino or Cora Cow. I wouldn't know where I was going. I might step in a puddle and get all wet. Of course, if I could lead the parade, it would have to go wherever I wanted it to go."

Rusty decided not to try to change Percy's mind about leading the parade. "We'll line up at noon. See you then."

Now Rusty was really beginning to worry. He had to think of some way to have the parade without disappointing any of his friends.

"**Hee-haw**-radly expected you'd have a parade and not ask me to join you," said a voice behind Rusty. He looked around and saw Damon Donkey looking down at him.

"Of course we want you in the parade," said Rusty quickly. "It'll be in the meadow at noon."

"I'll be there," declared Damon. He started to walk slowly away, then stopped and added, "Naturally, I must insist on leading the parade."

Rusty knew there was no use in arguing with stubborn Damon Donkey. What a problem! All he had wanted to do was lead a parade in the meadow on a bright summer day. Now he had five leaders and no parade.

Rusty flew to the top of the fence to figure out how to solve his problem. Suddenly, he had an idea! He wasn't sure it would work, but he would try it.

Rusty rushed to the meadow at noon. All of the other animals were already there. They were talking excitedly about the parade. Rusty flapped his wings to quiet them.

"Cock-a-doodle-doo! A cheery good afternoon to you," crowed Rusty. "Let's get in line. I'll show you to your places."

What a lot of excited neighing and mooing and oinking and quacking and hee-hawing there was as Rusty arranged the parade. When everyone was in place, Rusty shouted, "Go!"

The animals began to march. They didn't notice that Rusty had arranged them in a big circle and so far apart that each animal though he was leading all the others. Everyone was happy.

Rusty stood in the center of the circle, flapping his wings excitedly as he watched the parade go by. Seeing his friends so happy was better than leading the parade himself.

Chauncey Cat's Concert

By Joan Fehlberg

One night, while exploring the attic, Chauncey Cat came upon a wonderful treasure—a battered, dusty book. Its cover read: *How to Play the Piano in 25 Easy Lessons. Win Fame and Fortune! Astound Your Friends!*

"This is it!" Chauncey gasped. "My dream come true!"

Chauncey's secret longing was to become a concert pianist. As a kitten he had shown great promise, and his mother had entertained high hopes. Unfortunately, though, no music teacher would give piano lessons to a cat, and so Chauncey's brilliant career had ended without his learning to play a single tune.

But he still yearned to make music. The joy of his life was the magnificently carved grand piano that occupied the parlor of dear Miss Appleton, Chauncey's mistress. Even though old Miss Appleton had grown frightfully hard of hearing, she kept the piano because it reminded her of the old days when the room rang with music. Now, of course, since she could not hear it and nobody could play it, the piano was still and silent. In fact, it was such a peaceful place that Chauncey's best friend, Fennimore Mouse, had set up housekeeping in it.

From time to time (with Fennimore's permission) when Chauncey felt some talent coming on, he would run across the keys or plunk a note or two. The music was most unsatisfactory.

Now he slid the precious book down the attic stairs and into the parlor. Eagerly, he studied Lesson 1 and then practiced some fancy footwork on the keyboard. "I can do it!" he cried.

Fennimore Mouse rushed out of the piano, all in a dither at the noise. "My friend," apologized Chauncey, "I believe you will need to find a new place of residence. I have decided to become a concert pianist."

Fennimore examined the new book and agreed that he should not stand in the way of genius.

From then on, Chauncey was a dedicated musician. Every night when Miss Appleton retired, he leaped eagerly up to the piano bench and practiced, four hours at first, then five—sometimes more. He played scales, glissandos, double thirds, trills—and, with help from his back feet, arpeggios.

In the piano bench Chauncey found books of beautiful music, written by people with odd names—Rachmaninoff, Chopin, Bartok, Mozart, Bach, Beethoven, Mendelssohn. He loved them all. With a happy cat-smile on his face, he swayed and pounced, his paws rippling over the black and white keys.

"Very nice," Fennimore Mouse would call from below. It was now his job to pump the damper pedal up an down and offer criticism.

"That last run was very nice but you are forgetting the E-flat."

Sometimes, after a particularly tiring practice session, the two friends would stretch out on the carpet and discuss Chauncey's career. Chauncey believed he could be ready for a concert appearance by next fall if he worked hard.

Then something happened to change their plans. Fennimore heard about it first. "Miss Appleton has gone to an ear doctor," he exclaimed, waving his paw excitedly. "Tomorrow she is being fitted for a hearing aid. No more night practicing for you. You must go to the concert hall and audition tomorrow!"

The man at the concert hall was very kind, although he was not sure how to audition a cat. Chauncey tried to put him at ease. He introduced Fennimore. "This is my associate, critic, and pedal-pumper. We are entirely self-taught musicians."

They took their places at the piano and began to play their favorite piece. Fennimore closed his eyes and pumped with all his might. Chauncey played with all his heart.

When they had finished, the kind man took Chauncey by the paws. "That was a remarkable performance—for a cat," he said gently. "But I am sorry. It is not quite remarkable enough for a concert pianist. Go home. You can make the people there very happy with your music. A concert artist has a very hard life, you know."

Chauncey was heartsick. He walked slowly home with Fennimore, their whiskers sagging and their tails drooping. Chauncey could not speak until they were nearly home. "Oh, Fennimore," he began. A tear rolled down one furry cheek and onto a volume of Chopin waltzes. "I don't feel bad because I can't be a concert pianist. All that practice every night was too hard anyway. But you left your home in the piano. You helped me. I have let you down."

"Nonsense!" Fennimore patted him on the back. "Remember the fun we had playing together. That's the most important thing. We'll go home and play for ourselves!"

Not much later, Miss Appleton arrived home from the ear doctor, her new hearing aid working beautifully. Strains of piano music floated out the open window. She gasped when she threw open the door. Happy tears filled her eyes. There was Chauncey, swaying and pouncing, his paws rippling over the keys.

"Bravo!" she cried, applauding." You must play for the Literary Society next Tuesday. It will be just like the old days!"

"Fennimore was right," Chauncey said to himself as he launched into a Beethoven sonata. "Music is for making people happy."

THE BALL GAME

By Miriam A. Roland

It was a lovely day for a walk. The bears took a walk every day. Papa said that walking was great exercise, even for bears. Baby thought climbing trees was better.

The best part about the walks was that they went a different way each time. Baby wondered where they were going today. Papa never got lost. This time they ended up in a little village at the bottom of a mountain.

Baby Bear was learning to read. He was very good at signs. "There's a ball game today. It says BEARS VERSUS TIGERS. Could we go Papa? Please?"

Papa puckered his mouth and scratched his head. He always did that before making his most important decisions.

"I don't know, son. Tigers are fearsome cats. I don't see how we bears can win."

Suddenly, a man with a funny striped suit came running toward them. "You must be the new mascots. Our regulars quit. We can't win a game without them. Come along quickly. We have a nice seat for you right by the team. Don't worry about a thing. We'll tell you what to do."

Mama's mouth dropped open, but before she could utter a word, Papa said, "Yes, sir! Sounds like a real good time. We're happy to help you out." Then he whispered to Mama and Baby, "Just act like you know what you're doing. You heard what the man said. They need us. Don't worry about a thing."

The crowd clapped and cheered and started to chant, "Bears, Bears, Bears!" Then someone shouted, "Here come the Bears."

Baby looked and looked. He didn't see any bears. He saw men in funny striped suits. On the front of their shirts it said "Bears."

The man told Papa that it was time to go out and cheer. That was fun. They yelled and did cartwheels and flips. The Tigers had a mascot too. Anybody could see that he wasn't real. His body was too flabby and wrinkled. He could walk on only two legs.

It was a strange game. A man picked up a stick, and another man threw a ball at it.

The Tigers were standing out in the grass. They all wore a funny big glove. Baby couldn't understand why. Most of them never caught anything. He asked Papa about it, and he said that wearing the gloves was a mighty smart idea. It always paid to be prepared.

Next Baby started to watch a man with a mask. The poor man couldn't even stand straight most of the time. Baby knew his eyes were bad. Sometimes he would yell, "Ball one. Ball two." Sometimes the confused man even saw four balls. Baby looked and looked. He was sure there was only one. If the man with the stick saw four balls, too, he could take a walk down the path.

Mama said it was a shame that they ran around that path so much. It ruined the grass.

When the man threw the ball against the stick, the crowd clapped. The people clapped the most when three men ran around the path at once.

Sometimes when a player waited with the stick in his hands, the man who couldn't see would yell, "Strike!"

Mama got mad. She jumped up and shook her finger at the man. The people laughed. Papa told her to sit down. Mama didn't believe in striking anything.

When some of the men held the stick they didn't want to hit anything, either. The man with the mask made them sit down.

Suddenly, the game stopped, and a loud voice announced a seventh-inning stretch. The bears stood up to stretch. They did all the stretching exercises they knew. Nobody was paying attention. They all went for something to eat.

When the game started again, the man threw the ball and it hit the man who was holding the stick. Mama started to get up. Papa told her to sit down again. He said that the man who threw the ball had a very hard job. It was amazing that he hit the stick as often as he did. Anyway, the man who got hit wasn't hurt. He felt good enough to walk down the path.

When one team got tired of standing on the grass, they walked off and sat on a bench. Then the other team had to stand there. They took turns all night.

Finally, a man on the Bears team held the stick just right and the ball hit it with a *whack*. Then the ball flew high into the air. All the people stood up and cheered. Lights flashed words on a big wall. HOME RUN! The Bears team was jumping around and hugging each other. Now Papa jumped up. He said they'd better get going if they were going to run home. That's what the sign said, and that's what they were going to do.

They didn't talk much on the way home, though Papa said he had the game figured out in a few minutes. Baby just held on to his parents as they pulled him along. Most of the time his feet didn't hit the ground. Mama never said a word. She was probably still worried about the grass. The three bears were tired, but they didn't stop running. They were all out of breath by the time they got to their front door. Papa said the hardest part of the ball game was running home.

THE TALKATIVE SQUIRREL

By Phyllis Fair Cowell

On a limb about halfway up his tree, Jeffrey Squirrel chatted with Oslo Bird. They had been sitting in that same spot for hours while they talked about the weather, their trees, and just about everything—Jeffrey doing most of the talking.

Just before dark, Oslo shook his wings and got ready to leave.

"I'm sure glad you came by," said Jeffrey. "I don't get many visitors up here, and you know how I love to talk."

"Yes," laughed Oslo, "you're very good at that."

"It gets so lonely up here," Jeffrey sighed. He peeked over the edge of the limb to see if there might be someone else coming.

"You should move down closer to the ground," Oslo suggested. "You come down only to gather a few nuts. Then you scurry right back up your tree. You'll never have more company up here."

"I have thought of that," Jeffrey said. "But I've been living up here so long, I don't know anyone on the ground. Folks won't come to visit someone they don't even know."

"You need a way to attract them," Oslo said.

Then, with a flutter of his wings, Oslo chirped, "Open a shop! Everybody will come to a shop. You will meet all of the new folks and see a lot of your old friends, too."

Jeffrey's tail curled and his face brightened.

"That's a great idea!" he exclaimed. "I'll open a . . . barbershop. Barbers always talk to their customers."

The next day Jeffrey brought his scissors down to the ground and opened his barbershop. Things were going just fine with his first customer, Mr. Beaver. Jeffrey talked and talked as he clipped rapidly at Mr. Beaver's hair. But Jeffrey was no barber, and very soon Mr. Beaver felt a cool breeze on top of his head.

He jumped up from his seat and grabbed the bald spot Jeffrey had created.

"You're no barber!" he shouted, "and I'm going to make sure everyone knows it."

Mr. Beaver stomped off through the woods, mumbling to himself.

Jeffrey saw the day pass without another customer. Mr. Beaver must have spread the word, and Jeffrey knew it was useless to try to keep his barbershop open.

The next day Jeffrey's barbershop was gone. But in its place stood Jeffrey's tailor shop. Sewing and pressing would be his special services now.

Mrs. Rabbit was the first to arrive. She had a coat to be pressed. Jeffrey heated the iron and began to talk as he worked. Mrs. Rabbit was quite happy talking to Jeffrey until she saw smoke billowing from under the iron.

"You're burning my clothes!" she shouted, snatching the coat from the ironing board. "I will never come here again and neither will my friends."

Once again Jeffrey watched the day go by without another customer. He was sad and he was lonely as he closed the tailor shop.

This time Jeffrey decided to quit trying.

"I should have stayed in my tree," he mumbled as he scurried up the tree trunk. When he reached the first limb, a familiar voice came from behind a clump of leaves.

"You get three strikes before you are out."

"It's no use, Oslo. I just can't run a shop of any kind. Anyway, no one will even come near me now," Jeffrey moaned.

"I think you are wrong," Oslo said. Mr. Beaver was pretty angry about the haircut, but he told everybody how much he enjoyed talking with you. So did Mrs. Rabbit."

"But what good will that do? I can't open another shop. I can't do anything," Jeffrey cried.

"Everybody has *some* talent," Oslo insisted, but Jeffrey scampered past him and disappeared.

That night, Jeffrey tossed and turned in the hollow of his tree. Thinking about Oslo's words kept him awake half the night.

"What can I do? What can I do? What . . ." suddenly Jeffrey knew! He fell asleep with a smile on his face.

In the morning, a new shop opened at the tree.

Folks came from near and far. They sat in the shade, laughing and talking and eating the nuts Jeffrey set out. Mr. Beaver and Mrs. Rabbit were there with many of their friends.

Everyone was having a wonderful time.

Oslo fluttered by and perched next to Jeffrey.

"What a success!" he exclaimed. "But . . . what kind of shop is this?"

Jeffrey laughed and pointed to a sign.

The sign said:

CHATTER SHOP
A Community Meeting Place
Nuts and Conversation
Supplied by Jeffrey

"I decided to use my talents," Jeffrey said. I'm a very good talker, you know."

But I Don't Like Flies

By Trinka Enell

"But I don't like flies," Fabian Frog said when his mother set a breakfast dish of fried flies in front of him.

"All frogs like flies," said his mother.

"Not me," said Fabian. "Flies make me sick." He leaped away, then dove deep into the pond where no one could find him and make him eat flies.

"Flies!" he burbled. "Yuck!"

And he chased some minnows, tickled a small striped snail, lassoed a friendly water snake, and played hide-and-seek with a crawdad. But finally Fabian Frog ran out of breath and had to come up for air.

His father spotted him immediately. "Hurrumph!" he said. "I understand you refused to eat the fine breakfast your mother prepared for you."

"But it was flies," Fabian explained. "Flies make me sick."

"You'll eat what your mother puts in front of you, young Frog!"

"I can't eat flies!" Fabian said.

"And we can't give in to you!" his father cried. "Remember the old saying—'A spoiled frog has few friends.'"

"Friends or not, I can't eat flies!" Fabian cried. And he hopped away to find a hiding place under the lacy ferns in the mudbank, where no one could find him and make him eat flies, and he wouldn't have to come up for air.

Fabian's mother sighed. "Well, perhaps I can disguise the flies."

"Excellent idea!" said Fabian's father.

So, when Fabian decided he was too hungry to hide out under the ferns any longer and had to come home to eat, his mother was ready with a delicious-looking lunch of flies, disguised by a creamy dandelion and mushroom sauce.

"Eat up, dear," she said.

Fabian sniffed his lunch suspiciously. It didn't look like flies—it looked like creamy dandelion and mushroom sauce. And it didn't smell like flies, either. But something about it (maybe it was the little black specks floating in the sauce) sure made him think of flies . . . He took a small bite. It tasted exactly like flies.

"Yuck! Flies!" he yelled. He spit out the bite and leaped away.

"Now what?" his mother said.

"I don't know," said his father. "Perhaps Old Tortoise will have some ideas."

So Fabian's parents hopped around to the far side of the pond where Old Tortoise was dozing in the sun.

"Fabian won't eat flies," said his mother.

"Not even disguised flies," said his father. "He says flies make him sick."

"A frog who gets sick on flies?" Tortoise repeated. "Very unusual. Hmmm . . . I must think on this." He closed his eyes and thought, and thought and thought and thought.

He opened his eyes. "Have you asked him what he can eat?" he inquired.

Fabian's father and mother blinked in surprise. "Why, no," they said.

"Do so," said Tortoise, and he pulled his head into his shell and snapped it closed.

"Right!" said Fabian's father and mother. And at once they hopped back around to the pond and waited impatiently for their young Fabian to come home.

Finally, when the sun started to slide behind the trees, Fabian Frog hopped from his hiding place under the lacy ferns in the mudbank.

"I can't eat flies," he said first thing.

"Yes, young Frog," his father hurrumphed. "We understand that. And although we don't believe in spoiling young frogs—you know the old saying about spoiled frogs—we are concerned, and we don't want you to starve—"

"Oh, for tadpoles' sake!" Fabian's mother interrupted. "Just ask him!"

"Right!" said Fabian's father. "What kind of food *can* you eat, Fabian?"

"All kinds of things," Fabian said. "Beetles and spiders and worms and grasshoppers and crickets and sow bugs and slugs and moths and—"

"All that?" his mother exclaimed.

"Sure!" said Fabian. "I like plenty of things. It's only flies that make me sick."

Fabian's mother and father looked at each other. "Hurrumph!" said his father. "Why didn't you say so?"

"You never asked me," said Fabian. He grinned a big froggy grin. "So," he asked, "what's for dinner tonight?"

The 10th Annual Hog's Head Hoedown

By Darleen Bailey Beard

"Just think," Petunia Piglet sighed, looking into the clouds. "Me, going to the Tenth Annual Hog's Head Hoedown."

"Oh, Petunia. You can't go to that highfalutin hoedown uninvited," her sister Pearl scolded. "You need a personal invitation from Mrs. Wigglyton. And she wouldn't invite you. You're just a common hog."

Petunia flopped over on her side and glared at Pearl. "Every year I've dreamed of going, and this year nothing's going to stop me, invitation or not!"

That afternoon Petunia soaked in a warm mud bath. She rolled over and over in fresh clover, pin-curled her tail, and rubbed red possum berries on her lips. Then she took her new pink bonnet with the fluffy blue feather and placed it on her head.

"You're not really going to that high-society hoe-down dressed like that, are you?" Pearl asked, holding her belly and laughing.

"This is what every fashionable hog will be wearing," Petunia replied, tossing her snout in the air and strutting out the gate.

Petunia was feeling quite jaunty until she arrived at the grand entrance of the Hog's Head Hotel.

"Your invitation, madam?" a handsome, spotted doorhog asked, adjusting his bow tie.

Petunia was flustered for a moment, but she hadn't gotten all dressed up just to be stopped at the front door.

"Yoo-hoo!" she sang, waving over the doorhog's shoulder. When the doorhog turned to look, Petunia dashed into the hotel and started down the long, graceful staircase into the ballroom.

"Seize that hog!" the doorhog ordered, shaking his fists.

Petunia quickly hopped onto the banister and swooped on her belly into the crowd of gasping hogs. By the time she reached the bottom, she was going so fast she couldn't stop. She flew over the violinist and belly-flopped right into the punch bowl.

Petunia looked at the mess she had made. All of the guests were laughing, licking red slushy goo off each other's faces. Punch dripped from the chandelier and oozed down the velvet wallpaper.

Petunia slid slowly out of the slippery punch bowl. She pulled her dripping pink bonnet with the drooping blue feather down over her face and darted under a nearby tablecloth.

"I've never been so insulted," a voice shrieked. "Imagine, that hog crashing my hoedown!"

"Now Piggie-pie, try not to be upset," a kind voice replied.

Petunia poked her head out from under the tablecloth. There, right in front of her, sat Mrs. Wigglyton. Mayor Wigglyton sat next to his wife. Punch dripped off their snouts, splashing into their crystal cups.

Petunia knew there was no way to leave gracefully. It was too late for that. She got up and ran, but her shoe caught in the hem of Mrs. Wigglyton's evening gown and she heard a loud *r-r-rip!"*

"My gown!" Mrs. Wigglyton screamed. "It's that horrible hog again. Throw her out!" She huffed off to the ladies' room.

Hot tears of shame flooded Petunia's eyes. She ran up the stairs, out through the grand entrance, and sat on the hotel steps, crying.

"Don't cry," a kind voice said. Someone handed her a tissue.

Petunia looked up. There stood Mayor Wigglyton, smiling in his punch-spattered tuxedo.

"How can I not cry?" she asked. "I've ruined the Tenth Annual Hog's Head Hoedown. Now everybody who's anybody knows that I'm a nobody."

"Dear young piglet," Mayor Wigglyton said, sitting next to Petunia, "you've *made* the hoedown! Why, without you, it would have been just another of my wife's boring socials!"

"Really?" Petunia asked.

"Oh, yes," Mayor Wigglyton insisted. "Years ago, when she first started the annual hoedowns, all the boars brought their fiddles. The sows brought the tastiest slop in all of Hog's Head. Everyone was invited, even the young piglets."

"That sounds like fun," Petunia said, wiping her tears. "Acting high-society must be really boring compared to something like that."

"Yes, it is," the mayor replied, rubbing his chin. "And it's awfully hard to dance a good jig in this hot tuxedo." He unbuttoned his stiff white collar and threw down the bow tie. "Let's go back inside."

The spotted doorhog scratched his snout in amazement as Mayor Wigglyton escorted Petunia back through the grand entrance of the Hog's Head Hotel. "Announcing Mayor Wigglyton and Miss Petunia Piglet!" he shouted.

Petunia was surprised to see everyone so happy. All the men hogs had rolled up their pant legs, taken off their fancy jackets, and discarded their shoes. The women hogs had thrown aside their fashionable bonnets.

But as they reached the bottom of the stairs, Mrs. Wigglyton stormed out of the ladies' room in her torn evening gown. Her snout had been powdered, and she looked as though she had been crying.

"I'm so sorry for tearing your beautiful dress," Petunia blurted. "I'd better leave now."

Mrs. Wigglyton looked at all the happy faces. She looked at the abandoned shoes, jackets, and bonnets. Her scowl turned into a smile. "Don't leave!" she said, taking Petunia's arm. "I want you to stay. From now on, everyone's invited to the Annual Hog's Head Hoedowns."

All the guests jumped and shouted in delight. The violinist yanked off his bow tie and played a hoof-tappin' tune.

"Wahoo!" Mayor Wigglyton exclaimed. "Now we can have a real hoedown. Pull up the carpet.

Waiter, corncobs for everyone." Then he turned to Petunia. "May I have the first jig?"

"Why, yes. I'd be honored." Petunia blushed. *Wait until I tell Pearl. She'll never believe it!* she thought, frolicking across the dance floor and crashing into a heaping tray of corncobs.

BEGONIA'S EARRINGS

By Sally Lee

"That new rabbit that moved in down by the pond is the most unfriendly thing I have ever seen!" Begonia grumbled. She plopped her fluffy cottontail down under a tree next to Pansy.

"Do you mean Rose? She was friendly to me," Pansy said.

"Well, she wasn't friendly to me! I did my best backward somersault. I even twirled my ears in the air until they hurt. She didn't even notice!" Begonia grumbled.

"You just don't have what it takes to make friends," Pansy sighed. "It's too bad you don't have magic earrings like I do."

Begonia's ears shot up. "Magic earrings? What are those?"

"Just some special earrings that make people notice you, that's all," Pansy answered. "I have hundreds of them."

"Could I have some?" Begonia begged.

Pansy studied Begonia for a moment, then shook her head. "I can't give any away. I was just getting ready to sell them all."

"How much are you selling them for?" Begonia asked eagerly.

"They're worth a lot of money. You probably wouldn't have enough," Pansy answered.

"I have sixty-three cents at home in my bank," Begonia said.

"Really? That's amazing. That's exactly how much I'm selling my earrings for." Then Pansy stopped and shook her head. "But, I can't sell them to you."

"Why not?" Begonia cried.

"Because you always get angry when you buy things from me. You didn't like the magic carrot seeds you bought from me, remember?"

"That's because they turned into spinach," Begonia grumbled.

"That's what was magic about them," Pansy argued. "And what about the awful fuss you made over the jumping beans I sold you?"

"You said they would make me jump higher. But instead they just gave me a tummyache," Begonia complained.

"That's what I mean. You always complain about the things you buy."

"I won't complain this time," Begonia promised.

"Well . . . OK. I'll give you one more chance. Go home and get your money. I'll get the earrings."

Soon Begonia was back with her money. She saw Pansy coming down the path dragging a large bag behind her.

"Did you get the money?" Pansy asked.

"Of course," Begonia said holding out her paw.

Pansy dropped the bag and quickly took the money. "Have fun with your magic earrings," she said with a sly grin. Then she scurried down the path toward home.

Begonia opened the bag, which was bulging with earrings in every color of the rainbow. She picked out two sparkling red ones and clipped them onto her ears. "Those are perfect," she squealed. "But maybe one pair won't have enough magic to do the trick. I'd better wear them all just to make sure."

Begonia began clipping the earrings on as fast as she could. Soon she had them up and down both sides of her ears as neatly as crocodile teeth.

"Now I'm ready to hop to Rose's house," she said. But try as she might, Begonia couldn't move. Her ears were much too heavy.

"If I can just make three good hops, I'll be where Rose can see me," Begonia groaned. She crouched down, then leaped as hard as she could. Her back legs flew up into the air, but her head wouldn't budge. She landed upside down with her nose stuck in a clump of clover.

Poor Begonia! There she was with her legs kicking wildly in the air and her ears spread out on the ground like fancy airplane wings. Her fluffy tail waved in the breeze like a dandelion puff.

The animals who saw her started to giggle. Soon there were five rabbits, three squirrels, and a frog all rolling on the ground holding their sides from laughing so hard.

"Oh, crunchin' cabbages!" Begonia shouted angrily. She kicked and wiggled and squirmed around, but it did her no good. She was still stuck topsy-turvy in the clover.

Angry tears filled her eyes as she watched the animals run laughing into the woods. "I may have to spend the rest of my life upside down," she wailed.

Suddenly a hard shove from behind sent her sprawling to the ground. Begonia looked up. She saw Rose standing next to her. "What are you doing here?" Begonia said sniffing.

"You looked as if you needed some help," Rose said, smiling. Then she covered her face with her paws and tried to hide her giggles. "Excuse me for laughing. I've just never seen someone do anything so funny before."

"I guess I did look a little silly," Begonia said with a grin. "Would you mind helping me get these pinching earrings off? My poor white ears are starting to turn purple."

Rose began helping Begonia take off the earrings. "Begonia, can I be your friend?" she said shyly as she dropped a big yellow earring onto the ground.

Begonia looked surprised. "Of course! That's what I wanted in the first place."

"You did! Then how come you didn't say anything?" Rose asked.

"Because I feel funny talking to people I don't know. Why didn't you say anything to me?"

"For the same reason," Rose giggled. She looked at the large pile of earrings in front of her. "What are we going to do with these?"

Begonia thought a moment. "I know, we can decorate this tree with them."

"Good idea! I'm going to call it our Laughing Tree. Whenever I see it, I will remember how funny you looked, and I'll start laughing all over again."

As they were clipping the last earring to the tree, Pansy hopped by.

"Hi, Pansy," Begonia called out. "You finally sold me something good. These earrings really work like magic."

"They do?" Pansy said in surprise.

"You bet. They got Rose to be my friend, just like you said they would."

With that, Begonia took Rose's hand. They hopped off toward the pond leaving a puzzled Pansy behind.